Sackets Harbor Powder Monkey
The War of 1812

Hope Irvin Marston
with Burt Phillips

Hope Irvin Marston
Isaiah 40:31

CreateSpace

SACKETS HARBOR POWDER MONKEY
The War of 1812

Includes historical notes and bibliography.

ISBN: 978-0-9849935-1-2
ISBN-10: 0984993517

DEDICATION

To Connie, Gary, Robert and Jeannie.
Without your inspiration and expertise
this story would never have been told.

WHO'S WHO IN THE BATTLE

All of my characters were real people who played some part in the First Battle of Sackets Harbor.

Colonel Christopher Bellinger—An officer of the New York State Militia

Captain Elisha Camp—Leader of a militia artillery company at Sackets Harbor

Sophia Camp—Wife of Elisha Camp

Hugh Earl—Commander of the *Royal George*

Augustus Ford—Warrant Sailing Master and pilot, third in command, and responsible for the navigation and all matters regarding the sailing of the *Oneida*

Hart Massey—Customs Collector based at Cape Vincent

Rankin McMullin—Younger brother of Will McMullin

Will (William) McMullin—Sackets Harbor farmer who joined *Oneida*

Hugh Paul—A friend of the McMullins who joined *Oneida* the same day as Will and Rankin

Abner Pierce—Neighbor of the McMullins

Thomas D. Spicer—A local militiaman

Julius Terry—A local person of color known as Black Julius

Abby Vaughan—Wife of William Vaughan

William Vaughan—A prominent local citizen who served in *Oneida* for a few months in 1811

Henry Wells—Acting Lieutenant in *Oneida*

Lieutenant Melancthon T. Woolsey, U.S.N.— Captain of *Oneida*

Kingston

Wolfe Island

Saint Lawrence River

Cape Vincent

Charity Shoal

UPPER CANADA

UNITED STATES NEW YORK

Point Peninsula

Pillar Point

Black River Bay

Horse Island

Sackets Harbor

N

Galloo Island

Stony Island

July the 19th, 1812

Sackets Harbor, New York

Lake Ontario

Northern Frontier

Oswego Harbor

CHAPTER ONE

Discovery

Sackets Harbor, New York

Fall 1810

Dawn had not yet lightened the sky as young Rankin McMullin yawned, stretched his lanky legs, and mulled over what might happen before the day ended. When he crept out to the cliff that morning, he hoped to find the warship *Oneida* had arrived while the village slept. He had never seen a warship, and neither had many of the others in the village. He wanted to be the first to see this one. He smiled at his older brother Will sleeping soundly. He'd move about quietly, not to wake him. With catlike movements he pulled on his trousers, snatched up his shirt, and crept out of the cabin. The lone call of a Canada goose broke the silence of the tangerine sunrise as he streaked toward the cliffs above the lake.

Pale rays of sunlight ribboned the sky. His heart raced as he approached the water. He was already out of breath when the sight before him stopped him dead in his tracks. The *Oneida* lay quietly at anchor waiting for the village to come to life. She had slipped into the harbor while nobody was watching.

Rankin had not expected her to be so grand. Two huge masts towered above the main body of the brig. His jaw dropped to his chin. He moved closer, measuring the higher mast with his eye, from the deck to its top. It appeared every bit as tall as the 90-foot white pine he and Pa had helped their neighbor bring down.

Held fast by her huge cable, the enormous vessel rocked gently at anchor. A light breeze teased the lashings on the giant sails. Rankin closed his eyes and pictured them billowing like enormous blankets. His heart thumped and his mind raced. Wouldn't it be exciting to join her crew?

The first morning he'd slipped out before sunrise, Will chided him. "So what if she is here?" Yesterday he asked, "Are you getting a reward if you are the first one to see her in the harbor?"

Just one glance at the majestic *Oneida* filled Rankin with intense longing to join the ship's crew. The brig was coming to protect Sackets Harbor from an invasion by the British, and he was glad.

When he wasn't helping on the farm, Rankin sometimes hung around outside the tavern, listening to the villagers argue. Most of the men approved of the warship's coming. The previous day, however, he'd discovered that not everybody was pleased.

Abner Pierce, one of their neighbors, warned that it might not be a good thing. "Just what will that brig be doing till the war starts?" he asked.

"What if she stops our potash shipments to Kingston?" said another worried farmer. He pounded the bar with a clenched fist. "Where will we get the money we need to buy things we can't make for ourselves?"

Rankin didn't say a word—it wasn't his place to argue with grown men—but he mentally shrugged. Though every family in Sackets knew the government forbade trading with Canada, most every one of them broke that law. How would they survive if the *Oneida* stopped them? In his excitement over the coming of the brig, Rankin pushed that conversation aside.

For months the men in the tavern had talked of nothing but the coming war. During the past two weeks, they'd made wagers over the day the new U.S. Brig *Oneida* would arrive to protect their little village. Now that she was here, Rankin's longing to go aboard grew like a spreading fire in dry desert.

How old did he have to be to join the crew? He chewed his lips, pondering his own question. Probably older than ten, but he'd soon be eleven.

First chance he got, he'd find out.

Reluctantly he turned from the cliff and hurried home to spread the good news.

CHAPTER TWO

Sackets Harbor Smugglers

Fall 1809

For two years Rankin had been yammering to go along with Pa and Will when they smuggled their potash across the lake to Canada. Pa finally gave in and said they would take him on their final trip to Kingston. Ma refused to allow it until Pa convinced her that Rankin was strong enough to help should they run into trouble. Now as he remembered that trip a few months ago, chills slithered down his spine again. His heart pounded as fast as it did that day on the yawl.

The previous fall Rankin had helped Pa and Will burn the last of their trees that they had left to dry for a season. When the burning was finished, they poured water over the ashes to leach out the potash.

"Well, Rankin," Will said as they finished the task, "we'll never have to do that again." He frowned and then added, "We need to smuggle this one last load to Canada, as soon as possible."

"Breaking the law to sell our potash has always bothered me," Pa said, "but we've had no choice." He smiled at Ma. "After this trip we're done smuggling. He looked at Rankin as if he were measuring his height. "You're tall for your age, and you're strong enough to help with the barrels. We'll take you with us."

"At last!" said Rankin, grinning from ear to ear.

"We'll load up the night before so we can get an early start," Pa said.

Will gaped at him as though he were talking gibberish. "An early start? We're leaving in broad daylight? Do you want to get us killed?"

"Of course not," Pa said. "By leaving at dawn we should be well on our way to Kingston before any customs collector's cutter heads out on the lake." He paused and glanced at Rankin. "We'll put you to work on the yawl keeping the barrels under control."

They had gotten underway at daybreak without attracting the attention of the local soldiers who were supposed to be on watch against smuggling activities. As they neared Charity Shoal, southwest of Wolfe Island, Will spotted a sail heading their way. "Look," he said, pointing behind them.

Pa peered in that direction. "Now I see it!" He studied the sail for a few minutes. "You have good eyes, Will! H'm. Could be just another smuggler," he mused, "or a customs collector. Best to take no chances."

A customs collector! Rankin's face turned ashen. If they were caught, Pa would lose his potash and their yawl would be confiscated.

"Don't fret," Pa said. "I think we're far enough ahead to outdistance whoever it is."

Pa adjusted the sails to increase their speed and headed toward a passageway too shallow for a cutter to enter. With the new course and speed, the yawl began pitching more and corkscrewing through the waves. It took every bit of strength Pa could muster to keep her on course.

To make things worse, a rogue wave washed over them and loosened one of the potash barrels. "Take care of the tiller, Will," Pa shouted, "while I help Rankin catch that barrel."

In the struggle to keep the barrel from rolling overboard, Pa lost his footing on the wet deck. He slipped and jammed his right leg between the loose barrel and the bulwark. They secured the barrel, but he couldn't put his full weight on his leg. "Will," he said, "let Rankin give you a hand with the sails and get us into the cove as quickly as you can."

Once they felt the coast was clear, Will and Rankin guided the yawl back out into the lake. Pa rested his bruised leg against the barrels. Mid-afternoon they slipped into a secluded dock on the Kingston shore. Their Canadian receivers helped unload the barrels and handed Pa the agreed upon amount for his potash. He counted his money and secured it in his deerskin money belt.

Pa was relieved that they had delivered their cargo without trouble, but he still had grave concerns. "We have no clearance papers allowing us to be out here on the lake. We must avoid the customs collector on the way home."

Rankin's heart thudded again. They were still in danger.

Pa's leg pained him. Rankin had not recovered from his scare. Will was tired from the strain of eluding their pursuers and helping with the sails. "Couldn't we spend the night here and try another early morning start?" he asked.

"Good idea," Pa said.

They wrapped themselves in the heavy blankets they had stowed on board, settled down in the yawl, and went to sleep.

Just before daybreak they slipped out of Kingston, headed for home. All three stayed alert for other vessels on the lake. They arrived home in the early afternoon, grateful for having had the lake to themselves.

That final trip had left Pa with a crippled leg and Rankin with a determination to sail on a big ship.

Once they were safely home, Rankin forgot his fears. The trip had whetted his appetite for more adventures on the lake. He would never be satisfied until he joined the crew of a big ship like the *Oneida*.

CHAPTER THREE

A Disrupted Breakfast!

Fall 1810

"THE *ONEIDA* IS HERE!"

Rankin wrenched the door open so hard it crashed into the cabin wall with a mighty *thump.*

His mother nearly dropped the pot of porridge she was carrying to the breakfast table. "My goodness, Rankin!" she exclaimed. Her voice softened a bit. "I didn't know you were out there again this morning looking for that ship."

Rankin's booming shout had Will out of bed and hustling to the table. "Is she really here?" he asked. He tried to hide his excitement when the family sat down to eat, but that was hard to do as Rankin described the

Oneida.

"She's big!" he said, "an, and her masts are so tall that—"

Will interrupted him. "The men at the tavern say she sailed from Oswego with only ten seamen on board, besides the officers. A warship that big will need lots of recruits." He glanced at Pa and added, "I'd like to join up as soon as I kin."

Pa looked at him, paused, and then spoke. "Our land is cleared. The trees are burned. Potash sold." He sighed as if a heavy load had been lifted from his shoulders. "Our smuggling days are over. From now on, we'll get cash from selling extra wheat to our neighbors."

"Yah," said Will, "and they'll pay for it by continuing to smuggle their potash to Canada."

He sensed Pa was willing to let him go but hadn't said so yet.

"Though we're no longer involved, we have ta help put an end to those dang rules that force good people to break the law." Pa winced and rubbed his right thigh. "I'd sign on myself if it weren't for my game leg." He laid a hand on Will's shoulder. "You may go in my place."

While Pa and Will talked, Rankin squirmed in his seat. He wanted to go, too, and now was the time to ask. Before he could open his mouth, his father said, "Rankin can help me with the farm chores."

At Pa's words a strangled cry escaped Rankin's throat.

All eyes were drawn to him.

Ma was the first to speak. "What's the matter, Rankin?"

Rankin tried to tell her he wanted to sign up, too, but the words wouldn't come out. "I-wanna – I WANNA JINE UP, TOO," he blatted.

Ma gasped, shaking her head no. She was willing to let Will go, but not Rankin.

Will frowned. "Pa can't get around like he used to. With me joining up, he'll need your help with the wheat harvest."

Rankin raised and then lowered his shoulders in a huff and scowled. "I wanna do something more excitin' than grow wheat."

Ma did not budge. "You are only ten years old, Rankin."

Rankin clenched his teeth. He looked at Ma, then pleaded with Pa. "Din't I prove how strong I was when we was running from that revenue cutter? Don't you remember how I helped you when that barrel got loose?" He turned to his mother. "Please, Ma, let me go with Will when he

18

signs up."

Will stiffened at Rankin's badgering. "Just what do you think ten-year-olds do on a warship?"

Rankin had no idea, but he was tall and strong. "I'm almost eleven!" he said. "Besides, I'm the tallest ten-year-old in Sackets Harbor. There must be somethin' I kin do."

Will looked him in the eye. "Boys on warships are powder monkeys."

Rankin wrinkled his nose. "Powder monkeys? What do they do?"

Will hadn't known what they did until he heard the tavern talk. "During a battle, they carry gunpowder from down in the hold up to the guns on deck. If the brig is hit, they're apt to be blown up. When the guns are fired, the noise is deafening. The boys must deliver the powder and get away as fast as they can. If they don't they could be struck by flying splinters."

Ma shuddered at Will's words. She didn't want Rankin to have such a dangerous job.

Though he was sure Rankin was too young to enlist, Will knew he had his heart set on joining the crew. Why not take him along? Captain Woolsey would send him home. Ma would be relieved, and Pa would have the help he needed.

"If you let him go, I promise to look after him."

Ma closed her eyes and breathed in deeply several times. Then she spoke in a whisper.

"I don't want you to go, Rankin. I will permit it to help bring this awful problem with Great Britain to an end." She took another deep breath. "I'll pray the Lord will protect you both."

A huge grin spread across Rankin's face. Before he could say anything, Will added, "Don't get your hopes up. A warship doesn't need a lot of powder monkeys."

Rankin punched Will on the forearm. "I hope the captain needs at least one more."

Will returned the jab.

Time passed slowly for Rankin and Will along with the other men waiting for word from the *Oneida* so that they could join up. Mid-afternoon Captain Woolsey came ashore with his Sailing Master and pilot, Warrant Officer Augustus Ford. Five of their crew of ten were with them. They spoke with the men gathered in the tavern. However, they made no attempt to enlist anyone before returning to *Oneida*.

During the next several days half of the crew hung out in the tavern, making conversation with the villagers. They wandered about the area familiarizing themselves with the terrain, and then returned to the brig, having said nothing about needing recruits. The next day they hauled in their anchor and returned to Oswego. They left behind dozens of puzzled, disappointed men, along with Rankin and Will McMullin.

Nothing was seen nor heard of Captain Woolsey or the *Oneida* until the next summer when she again slipped into the harbor unnoticed. When her presence was discovered, again the men congregated in the tavern. Many of them held high hopes of becoming part of her crew. Mid-morning a messenger from the *Oneida* brought word that Captain Woolsey was putting out a call for recruits. Anyone interested in joining his crew should report to him the following Friday, June 21, 1811.

CHAPTER FOUR

Face to Face with Captain Woolsey

Late June 1811

The day had finally come. Rankin was so excited he scarcely tasted his porridge. Wild horses couldn't have stopped him or Will from scrambling down the hill to where the U.S. Brig *Oneida* rode at anchor. Rankin's dream of joining the ship's crew grew with each step he took toward the warship. He hoped his long legs and strong muscles would make up for the fact that he was not quite twelve years old. When they were close enough to hear the gentle waves slapping the sides of the warship, he saw the captain, Lieutenant Melancthon T. Woolsey, standing on deck. He was stroking the binnacle as he scanned his surroundings.

Captain Woolsey stilled his hand and focused on the two men

heading down the hill. One seemed to be in a hurry, and he appeared to be a head shorter than the other. Shorter and younger, but looking lean and strong like his companion.

Were they coming to join his skeleton crew of "iron men"? He hoped so. His brig was sound but short-handed. He needed men with muscle to work the ship and man the guns. He must recruit a full crew as quickly as possible and prepare them for the impending war. They'd get their training by running down smugglers who sneaked their potash across Lake Ontario to Canada whenever they thought the coast was clear.

As soon as he thought the men were within earshot, Captain Woolsey hailed them. He pointed to a boat pulled up on the shore. "Take that skiff and come aboard."

They did so. Right smartly, too. Obviously they were no strangers to the water.

"I'm Rankin McMullin, Sir," the younger one blurted out as soon as they were on deck. "This is my brother Will. We've come to sign on your ship."

The captain cast a glance at Will and then studied Rankin's face. He was obviously much younger than his brother. But he had mettle, and he was clearly seasoned by work. He might make a good powder monkey, despite his height. Why not question him first?

Rankin held his head high as Captain Woolsey pierced him with dark eyes.

"Rankin? You said that's your name?" Before Rankin could answer, the captain added, "Why do you want to join my vessel?"

"Sir," Rankin sputtered, "I want tuh be a powder monkey. "

"How old are you?"

"Twelve, Sir!"

Will gasped. Rankin wouldn't be twelve until September.

Woolsey sized him up. He had judged him to be several years older. With those long legs, the lad could cover distance in a hurry. He'd learn to duck his head after he thwacked it a couple of times rushing up from below deck. The captain pursed his lips. The lad was spunky, but not cocky. He liked that. But how would he react under fire? Intending to test him, Woolsey stared him in the eyes.

Rankin stared back.

"Warships need boys to carry powder charges from the magazine down in the hold up to the carronades on deck. If they don't get the charges to the guns, the fight is lost." He kept his eyes focused on Rankin. "Things get pretty messy during a battle. You can't faint at the sight of spattering blood and guts when a man gets hit!"

Rankin didn't scare easily. He shoved his hair back from his forehead and remained unmoved.

The captain continued. "It we take a hit by a ball, you could be stabbed by flying wood splinters nearly as big as oars.

Rankin still didn't flinch.

"Doesn't that frighten you?"

"A mite, Sir." Rankin spoke calmly. "But I'd risk it to become a member of your crew."

Captain Woolsey picked up a dry quill from his desk and twirled it between his thumb and forefinger. "I need another powder boy," he said.

Rankin twitched. Was the captain going to accept him? Or send him home?

After what seemed like a very long time, Captain Woolsey said, "I can use you." He handed him the quill and nodded toward the open ledger on his desk. "Make your mark there."

"Thank'ee, Sir."

Rankin flashed an I-knew-I'd-get-accepted look at his brother, took the quill, dipped it into the ink and wrote his name.

The captain's eyes widened in surprise. The kid could write!

Rankin hid his excitement as best he could as he put the quill back into the bottle.

Captain Woolsey palmed his chin and turned his attention to Will. "Why do you want to be a part of my crew?"

Will straightened his shoulders, and his muscles bulged under his homespun shirt. "Sir," he said, his voice loud and tinged with pent up anger, "the British have shoved us around far too long! Everyone knows we're going to be fighting them one of these days! That day can't come soon enough for me!"

The captain's eyebrows jumped at the man's outburst. "Great Britain *has* provoked us," he said. "She's kidnapped our sailors and pressed them to work on the King's vessels." Frown lines creased his forehead. "Now she's blocked us from trading with Europe."

"Aye, Sir." Will nearly interrupted the captain. "Then our government passed embargos to get back at them. For the past five years, we've had to smuggle our potash across the lake to sell it." He scratched his head as if to vent his frustration. "We'd starve if we didn't!"

Rankin shot him a warning glance, but Will's complaints continued to pour out like a raging river overflowing its banks. "They pay us well, and it's a good thing they do. Potash is our only source of cash. Nobody is going to keep us from trading with Cana—"

Rankin jabbed him in the ribs.

The captain covered his mouth with the palm of his hand. He understood Will's complaints. Sympathized with them, in fact. However, once he had a full crew, their work would be to run down smugglers just like Will and his neighbors. He was aware that nearly every farmer in Jefferson County made potash and smuggled it to Canada. That made Sackets Harbor men experts in avoiding rocks and shoals. They'd be an asset when patrolling the lake.

"My brig is here to defend your village when the British launch their attack," Captain Woolsey said. "Until that happens, my assignment is to enforce the embargo against trading with Canada."

Will rolled his eyes heavenward and inhaled deeply, but he said nothing.

The captain continued. "I need a crew of men with fire in their bellies and steel in their backbones."

He rested his hand on his hip. He'd have to take his chances with smugglers like Will McMullin. He hoped he could trust them to obey orders when *Oneida* was chasing their neighbors.

"The British want control of Lake Ontario, but they'll never get it!" He clenched his fist and slammed it against the binnacle. "We'll drive them out of Canada before they try."

"Sir, I can see that your guns are ready for that action!"

Captain Woolsey's eyes widened. "What do you know about guns?"

"Sir, I apprenticed with a gunsmith back in Connecticut before we moved west." He looked straight at the captain. "I can take care of your great guns and your small ones."

Woolsey nodded toward his desk and the open ledger. "Make your mark there! We need an armourer."

Will picked up the quill and wrote his full name just as Rankin had done.

Captain Woolsey's eyebrows arched upward once more. His new armourer could write, too! He checked his shrug before it became visible."Report to me in two days."

"Thank you, Sir," said Will.

CHAPTER FIVE

On Board at Last

Two days later

Not knowing when he would see his sons again, Pa had kept them busy with things he couldn't do himself after they were gone. Ma hustled about the house, discomposed at the thought of her boys leaving. She would miss them terribly, but she was proud of them for wanting to go.

Though they had no idea what life on the *Oneida* would be like, Rankin and Will looked forward to it. They said their hasty "goodbyes" and headed down to the lake. When they arrived, they discovered a gangplank had been laid in preparation for the men reporting for duty. They strode across the bridge-like structure and disappeared into *Oneida*.

After signing on a few more men, the *Oneida* put out on the lake so the old salts could teach the newcomers. First they'd show them how to handle the sails and then watch as they worked them on their own. They would teach them about the guns in the same way.

Rankin and Will had been on board for scarcely an hour when a sailor grabbed Rankin by the arm. "You're needed to help scrub the bilges," he growled. He yanked him toward the hatch and half dragged him down the ladders beyond the lower deck to the hold.

Rankin's heart thundered against his chest as though it were trying to escape his body. His eyes watered. He glanced about to see what stunk. With only the light of the oil lamps softening the darkness, everything appeared shadowy. The stench grew stronger as he was led around cannonballs, ropes, what might be food supplies and water barrels, toward the lowest part of the ship, the bilges. Never had he smelled anything so foul. The strong odor of vinegar made it even worse. He clapped his free hand over his mouth and held his breath as long as he could. Then he puked.

His burly escort cursed under his breath but hung on to his arm.

Rankin gulped in another breath of the fetid air and a second eruption followed. He brushed himself off as best he could with his free hand.

When they reached the bilges, his captor nodded toward several crew members scrubbing with about as much vigor as sleeping turtles. In the dimness of the hold, the men appeared dark skinned. Maybe they were just dirty. They worked in silence at their distasteful assignment.

"Grab that swab over there," said Rankin's captor, sounding like a judge sentencing him to the gallows. He let go of Rankin's arm and nudged him toward the corner. "Don't be a slacker," he warned, "unless you want to spend all your watches down here with the rats!"

Rats? Rankin grimaced. Was he referring to the men? Or to rodents? He covered his nose with one hand and steadied himself with the other as he edged his way toward the corner. When he reached the swab, he held his breath as long as he could, picked it up, and moved back to join the men already at work. Before long his shoulders began to ache from this unaccustomed duty.

He peered at the others through the semi-darkness, trying to read the expressions on their silent faces. Were they friendly fellows, he wondered.

Were they too tired to talk? Or did they need every ounce of energy to scrub away that awful stink?

Rankin pondered his plight as he scrubbed along with the speechless men. He had signed up to be a powder monkey, not to work in this wretched dungeon. How did he end up here?

Was this a test of his endurance? Maybe it was designed to see if he could follow orders. Those other weary men would have been raw recruits once upon a time, just as he was today. Was this work their punishment for something they had done?

No one had told him powder monkeys had to work like slaves in stinking bilges that made them puke. He grimaced and sighed. He'd do his best to keep up with the other men. If they spoke well of him, maybe he wouldn't be sent back here again.

His thoughts were interrupted by the man scrubbing near him. "Hey, kid! Stop your daydreaming, and keep that swab moving!" He nodded to the right. "Them barrels over there hold our drinking water. If we don't get these bilges cleaned and sweetened with the vinegar, the stink will seep right into them."

"Yeah," said another voice in the semi-darkness, "and if we kin get 'em smelling clean-like, maybe the rats won't like it and will move out!"

The other men guffawed, but Rankin shuddered. Thus far he hadn't seen a rat, but that didn't mean they weren't around. Trying not to inhale, he scrubbed faster and harder, hoping to keep them away from where he was working if they were somewhere close by.

BONG-BONG! BONG-BONG! BONG-BONG! BONG-BONG!

The sound of bells echoed down from the upper deck. Rankin peered at the others to see what that meant. By the time the last bell died out, several men had tramped down the ladders.

The forenoon watch had ended.

One by one the newcomers picked up the gear left by their weary crew mates, who seemed to have no energy left to express their relief.

Rankin scuttled away from the stink hole and clambered up the ladders behind the others. When he reached the deck, he gulped in the fresh air. Weary and nearly blinded by the light, he collapsed.

Will found him fast asleep, curled up on the deck. He shook him awake. "Come on," he said, "it's time eat." He took him down to the berthing compartment on the first deck where about a dozen seamen sat around a table. "Each group is called a mess," he explained. "These men are our messmates."

Will had learned a lot while Rankin was working in the bilges. He pointed toward two empty places on the far side of the table.

They moved into them and nodded toward the others. Rankin, still feeling the effects of his morning assignment, looked at his bowl of pea soup and then at the chunk of salt pork. His mother's food looked much more inviting. He took one taste and laid down his spoon.

After the meal ended, Will explained what he'd been doing during the forenoon watch. "The warrant officer in charge of the guns and the powder is called the Gunner," he said. "When he found out I was an armourer, he set me to work tuning up the firelocks on the muskets." Will flexed his arm muscles as if to relax them and glanced toward the big guns. "During my next watch I'm supposed to begin scraping the rust off the carronades." He drew in a long breath and let it out slowly. "It'll take a lot of work to scrape just one of them, and I counted nine on each side." He paused until Rankin looked him in the eye and then added, "I asked the

Gunner if you could work with me."

Rankin's eyes widened. "What did he say?"

"Since he's in charge of all the powder boys, he said that would be all right, that you'd have plenty of time to learn your duties."

Rankin's grin spread from ear to ear. "Anything is better than going back to those stinkin' bilges."

Later in the day the new crew members were assigned hammocks. That night they were shown how to unroll them and sling them from iron hooks set in the ceiling above them. The hard part was learning to get into them. After a few practice leaps, Rankin made a perfect landing.

Will applauded.

In time the two of them would master leaping into them with ease, and they'd soon learn to sleep comfortably thereafter. Still, it seemed strange to sleep in the same place where they had eaten. He shrugged.

Space is limited on a warship.

CHAPTER SIX

Lessons from the Gunner

Summer 1811

During the next few days Rankin was assigned menial tasks on board. He didn't mind emptying the ashes or the garbage from the galley. He watched the others to learn how to properly swab the deck. One of the crew members showed him how to polish the ship's bell and the binnacle until he could see his face in them.

One afternoon watch he was again set to helping Will scrape rust from the brig's many carronades. "I've been at this job most of my watches since we came on board," Will said.

Rankin looked at the carronade and whistled. "How long is that gun?"

"About four feet." Will rolled his shoulders. "I hope we can get all the carronades cleaned up and blackened before the British attack us."

Scraping rust didn't look like much fun, but so what? He could wait a few days until somebody showed him what his powder monkey duties would be. Rankin drew in a big breath and set to work beside his brother.

For the next week or so the brothers worked together cleaning the carronades. Will explained the routine on the vessel and the duties Rankin might have along with several other powder boys on board.

They had been on the *Oneida* about a month when one of the crew showed him how and when to turn the hourglass. "It takes exactly a half hour for the sand to pass through from top to bottom," he said. "Watch it carefully. Turn it over as soon as the last bit of sand disappears from the top. Then strike the bell." He showed him the lanyard attached to the clapper of the bell, then glanced at the hourglass. It was time. "Here's how to do it."

He seized the lanyard and gave it a yank.

BONG! The bell ran out, loud and clear.

"The second time you turn the hourglass, strike it twice."

Rankin listened intently as the sailor told him how to strike the bells during a four-hour period with brief pauses after each hour.

"Four hours is the length of a watch," he said.

Rankin understood the pattern and practiced his way through it, tapping on the rail.

Thump.

Thump-Thump.

Thump-Thump. Thump.

Thump-Thump. Thump-Thump.

Thump-Thump. Thump-Thump. Thump.

Thump-Thump. Thump-Thump. Thump-Thump.

Thump-Thump. Thump-Thump. Thump-Thump. Thump.

Thump-Thump. Thump-Thump. Thump-Thump. Thump-Thump.

His instructor grinned. "Perfect!" he said. "On your next watch, this will be your job. I'll be right there with you." He gave Rankin a gentle poke on the shoulder. "Do it right the first time, and that'll be your assignment whenever you're on watch. That job sure beats hauling on lines or going aloft in a storm."

Rankin returned to the carronades smiling. His voice bubbled as he told Will what he'd learned. "Turning the glass will be more fun than emptying garbage or polishing the binnacle."After his initial burst of enthusiasm, he said no more.

Will paused in his scraping and looked at him. Rankin's face had lost its glow, and his lips were sealed. Will dropped his tools and laid a hand on his shoulder. "What's bothering you?"

Rankin raised his shoulders and then dropped them with a sigh. "I jined up so's I could be a powder monkey," he said. "Why is the Gunner giving me these other jobs? When's he gonna show me what powder boys do? When will I learn to run up and down the ladders carrying powder to the carronades? Who's gonna—"

Will raised his hand palm outward to stop Rankin's rant. "Look, Rankin. There's a lot to be done to keep this brig running. Every job is important. The Gunner knows you're here to be a powder monkey. He'll show you what to do once you can handle all these other things."

"Yes, but why—"

Will silenced him again. "Just do what you are told, when you are told, and the best you can. Now stop complaining." He turned back to his work. "I'm almost finished with this gun. If you help me, it will be done by the end of the watch."

Rankin gritted his teeth and set to work. He'd do his best and try not to complain…too loudly.

It was almost the end of the watch when the Gunner showed up. Neither Will nor Rankin realized he had been standing close enough to observe them at work. He smiled as he watched them check for any speck of rust they might have missed before they quit.

"That's it, Rankin," Will said after examining the last inch of the carronade. "There's another one ready to be blackened."

At that moment the Gunner made his presence known. "Well done, men." He looked directly at Rankin. "You seem to enjoy working around the guns," he said. "I understand you do whatever is assigned to you. You do it well and you don't grumble about it." He cleared his throat. "I haven't forgotten you are the new powder monkey on board. I'll be showing you those duties one of these days. Meanwhile, I have another job for you."

Rankin stared at him, not knowing what to expect. Please don't let it be a boring job.

"Before we engage in any action, we have to put the powder into flannel bags to make up the charges," the Gunner said. "We store the powder in the magazine down in the hold behind a wet curtain. Tomorrow during the forenoon watch, you'll help me with that job."

Rankin's chest nearly burst with pride. "Aye, aye, sir," he answered in a voice so excited it squeaked. He dropped his head in embarrassment.

The Gunner flashed Will a broad smile and returned to his duties elsewhere.

That evening when the men pulled down their hammocks from where they'd been stowed, Rankin's thoughts flew toward the next day's activities. By now getting into his hammock was as easy as it was tricing it up each morning. Being a member of Captain Woolsey's crew was a good life. He looked forward to learning more about a powder boy's duties. He fell asleep wondering what tomorrow would bring.

In his dreams Rankin re-lived his first days on board the *Oneida*. Will had introduced him to their messmates, and they soon became close friends. That hadn't kept them from making him the butt of some of their pranks. Like sending him to get "50 feet of waterline" from the bos'n. None of their pranks were harmful. He soon realized he was being tricked because he was the youngest crew member. He accepted that with good humor. The men would not deliberately put him in danger.

When he awakened, he momentarily forgot where he was. Then it came back to him, along with thoughts of his first night leaping into the hammock and trying to get comfortable. He'd mastered that without too much difficulty. Now he slept well, swinging gently from the hooks as the ship rolled through the waves. He slowly unfolded himself, dropped to the deck, and stowed his hammock. Today he'd help the Gunner and just maybe he could find out more about his powder boy duties. He was eager for breakfast and anxious to begin his new assignment.

When the bells called the crew to work, Rankin hurried down the narrow gangways and dimly lit ladders to the handling chamber. He pushed his way through a wet curtain and found the Gunner already there.

As if he'd read his mind, the Gunner said, "We don't want to blow up our own ship. The wet curtain reduces the risk of an explosion." He looked at Rankin, nodded toward a room on his left, and spoke in measured words. "We store the barrels of powder in the magazine, as far from the carronades as possible. One of my gunner's mates will bring the powder to us. We'll measure out the exact amount for a charge and pour it into a flannel bag. Then we'll tie the bag and stack the charge in this locker. When we go into battle, my gunner's mate will pass a leathern bucket filled with charges to you through the wet curtain."

He looked directly into Rankin's eyes. "You understand what might happen when you dash up there carrying a bucket of powder, don't you?"

"Aye, sir."

"The deck is no place for the timid during an attack. The roar of the big guns will deafen you. Soot will blacken your face. Flying splinters can put out your eye or pierce your heart." He lowered his voice. "You need a strong stomach. When men take a hit, it gets messy." He looked at Rankin's shoes. "A bloody deck is slippery. You need to run in your bare feet for safety and speed. You must keep the powder dry. You take it to the guns assigned to you. Then you get out of there as fast as possible."

He placed a firm hand on one of Rankin's shoulders. "Captain Woolsey says you didn't flinch when he explained these things to you.

With a brave lad like you delivering the powder, we'll be ready to fight." He squeezed Rankin's shoulder ever so lightly. "Just don't get yourself killed."

At that moment one of the crew members peeked through the wet canvas. The Gunner nodded, and he entered the chamber carrying two leather buckets. The Gunner took them from him and set them on a low table. The gunner's mate returned with an opened keg of powder, which he placed next to the buckets. Kneeling beside the table, the Gunner said to Rankin, "I'll show you how to tie up the bags and then we'll get to work."

He measured out a precise amount of powder. "Hold the bag open so I can fill it." Once the bag was filled, he twisted string around the top and secured it with a strong knot. "Now you tie this next one like I showed you," he said.

Rankin took the string and tied it, under the Gunner's watchful eyes.

The Gunner smiled. "Good job. Next time while you tie one bag, I'll measure out the next charge."

Within a short time the two coordinated their efforts and the number of filled charges grew. By the time the bells ended the watch, the charges were stowed safely back in the magazine, lined up as precisely as soldiers in battle formation.

Rankin followed the Gunner topside, satisfied that his work was part of preparation for battle. He liked working with the Gunner and at last, he'd been given some powder boy instructions. He drew in a long breath and exhaled as slowly as he could. He had learned a lot today.

Now that he knew what to expect, he'd get in shape dashing up and down those ladders and narrow gangways. He'd have to be careful not to whack his head.

Being a powder monkey on the *Oneida* was certainly more exciting than chopping trees, setting them afire, and leaching potash from the ashes. Or raising wheat.

CHAPTER SEVEN

Winter Activities

Late fall 1811

The ship's crew continued their training exercises on the lake until ice began to form. Then *Oneida* was laid up at Sackets Harbor for the winter and her crew housed on shore.

During her first winter in Oswego, ice had pushed the brig off its moorings. When spring came, it took two months of backbreaking labor to get her back into the water. Then she had to be refitted. "That's why I insisted on making Sackets Harbor her homeport," Captain Woolsey said as he discussed his plans with Lieutenant Wells. "We'll see that she is well protected here."

Lieutenant Wells nodded. "We'll take down her rigging on the next watch."

"Put one section to work removing everything that might freeze."

"Beg pardon, Sir, but where shall we stow our stores?"

Captain Woolsey nodded toward a small blockhouse on the north shore. "When government troops were sent here to enforce the embargo, they built that blockhouse. We've received permission to use it."

"Aye."

"Once the ice becomes solid enough, the British may try sending troops across the lake from Kingston," said the captain. "We need to protect the brig as well as stand against an attack." He paused as if he were pondering how to do that. "Divide your men into three watches, each with four sections."

Wells surmised what Captain Woolsey was thinking. "That will enable us to protect ourselves from winter's ravages and local pillage and vandalism, won't it?" he said.

The captain agreed. "Assign one section to keep the snow off the decks and a second to chop the ice surrounding the hull so it won't

48

damage the brig. Have the third section post lookouts for anyone approaching, especially at night. The fourth will protect the brig from plunder."

By mid-March the ice was gone, and Lake Ontario opened for navigation. The crew re-rigged the brig and prepared her to return to service. They cleaned her decks, re-tarred the rigging, and bent on the sails that had been newly made or repaired over the winter.

Once their preparations were completed, they put out again into the lake each day for more sail-handling practice and gun drills.

One morning Rankin and Will learned that *Oneida* was going to patrol the lake in search of smugglers. Thoughts of that final trip when they had eluded a customs collector's cutter chilled Rankin, like a fall through the ice. He blanched at the thought of *Oneida* pursuing one of their neighbors.

When they found a few minutes to be alone, Will tried to calm him. "Stop fretting," he said. "We didn't get caught, and neither will they."

Later, when they were out in the middle of the lake, Will kept his eyes peeled for action on the water. Mid-morning he discovered they were not alone. He focused on what looked like a sail. Was it another smuggler? Or a customs collector?

Shortly thereafter the lookout spotted the sail. The vessel was heading their way on almost the same course and slowly gaining on them.

Oneida altered her course to intercept her.

Will studied the vessel as they moved closer to each other. Before long he recognized the mottled sails of their neighbor's sloop. He found Rankin and spoke quietly to him.

"It's Abner Pierce," he said. "When he realizes he's been seen, he'll disappear just as we did when we were chased!"

Rankin relaxed a bit, but not completely, until their prey had vanished from the lake.

"I'm glad Pa doesn't have to smuggle any more potash to Kingston," he said. "I hate the way the British mistreat us." He looked at Will and added, "I want this war to start soon and put an end to that!

CHAPTER EIGHT

Preparing for War

Spring 1812

KNOCK-KNOCK!

"Come."

"You sent for me, Sir?"

"Yes, Henry, come in. Take a seat."

Captain Woolsey seated himself opposite his lieutenant. "It's time to tell you the overall plans for invading Canada," he said as he made himself comfortable. "The United States intends to launch surprise attacks on three fronts. On Lake Champlain. From across the Niagara River. And across from Detroit." He squared his shoulders and looked toward the unseen bluff. "Here on the Northern Frontier we'll be in the midst of the action."

"Sir, what are your immediate plans?"

"We are prepared for action," said the captain. "We need to inform our men of our present situation." He stood and donned his coat. "Have the crew called to quarters. I'll be up in a moment."

Pipes sounded. Petty officers shouted. The men hastily lined up in orderly ranks in front of the binnacle.

Captain Woolsey emerged on deck, buckling his sword belt. He wasted no time in stating his business. "Gather round, men, I have news."

The excited crew broke ranks and came closer.

"The British have built more vessels since they launched the *Royal George*. I'm certain they have their eyes on *Oneida*. We can expect them to attack at any moment."

Rankin began to twitch as though he'd just sat on an ant hill. "I'm gonna do what I been practicin'," he whispered.

Will grinned and put his finger to his lips.

"Last spring the schooner *Julia* was launched in Oswego," the captain said. "I'm having her bring the 32-pounder long gun originally intended for *Oneida* to Sackets Harbor."

Will McMullin's eyebrows shot upward. A 32-pounder? It would be about ten feet long!

Augustus Ford whistled. "That gun must weigh at least three tons!" He shook his head at the thought of using such a weapon. "One ball from that beauty could sink a schooner!"

Captain Woolsey smiled. "That's what I'm intending." Turning to Lieutenant Wells, he ordered, "Dismiss the men."

The two officers remained on the quarterdeck. Speaking as much to himself as to his lieutenant, Captain Woolsey said, "At this point I don't know just how I'll use the *Julia,* or the long gun. But mark my words! We'll be glad we have them once the fighting starts."

In mid-April customs collector Hart Massey had spoken with Captain Woolsey about smuggling on Lake Ontario. "I suggest you watch for any vessels heading toward Cape Vincent," he said. "Goods shipped there is bound for the illegal Canadian market at Montreal or Kingston."

On June 3rd Woolsey and his 88-man crew sailed out of Sackets Harbor in search of smugglers. The next day they spied three vessels on the lake. They gave chase, but the wind dropped. Darkness came on. They had to wait out the night under short sail.

At daybreak, they discovered two schooners making toward the American shore.

"Sir, shall we go after them?" Lieutenant Wells asked.

Captain Woolsey nodded. "We'll overhaul them, board, and get ourselves a couple of prizes!"

The brothers were within earshot of the captain's plans. "Prizes?" Rankin said. "What kinda prizes is he talkin' about?"

Will flashed him a knowing smile. "Prizes means money. For everybody. A captured ship and its goods are sold. The money goes to the crew that captured it."

Rankin's eyes nearly popped out of his head. "Will I git some of it?"

"Yes, you will! It's divided up according to rank. Everybody gets a share."

Captain Woolsey could see Rankin was itching for a battle. This time he just might get it. Before the day ended, he could be flying up from the magazine toting charges of powder. The gun crews had praised his speed as he'd practiced his duties. It looked like his courage under fire would soon be tested.

Oneida pursued the schooners. One of them got away, but they caught up with the other one around 7: 00 p.m. "It's the *Lord Nelson*," said Captain Woolsey. "As soon as we are in range, I'll fire a warning shot." He turned to Rankin. "We need powder!"

Rankin whipped around, bounded down the ladders to the magazine, and grabbed the leather bucket of charges held out to him. At last he was doing what he'd enlisted to do. He raced back on deck and handed the powder bags off to the gun crew. Then he stood back out of the way to watch the action.

Oneida altered course slightly to bring a gun to bear.

"Fire!"

The ball flew across *Lord Nelson's* bow, sending up a mighty splash on the other side.

It was a warning not to be ignored.

Lord Nelson turned into the wind and hove to. Lieutenant Wells led an armed boat crew in boarding the Canadian schooner. Once on board, he demanded that the captain, who was an American citizen, show him her papers. She had nothing except a journal and a bill of lading of part of her cargo.

Captain Woolsey suspected her intention was to smuggle both ways. He took control of her. "She's our prize," he said. "Mr. Wells, detail some hands to take her to Sackets Harbor. The vessel will be sold to the Navy." He chuckled. "The government will pay us prize money, and we'll refit her as a warship."

Rankin frowned when no battle ensured. "Ain't we ever gonna have a real fight?" he muttered.

The *Oneida* continued to sail the waters of Lake Ontario daily, looking for illegal activity. Captain Woolsey insisted his men and his brig be ready for the war they all knew was coming. While Lieutenant Wells drilled some sections of the crew for combat, the others took care of the normal wear and tear on the vessel. Some men greased the blocks to make it easier to handle the sails. Some re-tarred the rigging and oiled the masts to protect them from the weather. Some pumped the vessel daily. Then they switched jobs, so that all of the men would be well trained.

Of course, everybody worked to keep the warship clean.

When Rankin's watch went on duty, his job was to mark the passage of time. Every thirty minutes he turned the hourglass. Then he struck the ship's bell to let the crew know what time it was.

One morning as he watched the sand moving through the glass, he overheard the men talking about the coming war. Their enthusiasm for the long gun captured his attention.

Later in the day he complained to his brother. "I didn't expect being a powder monkey to be so borin'! I don't mind watchin' the glass. I like strikin' the bells to tell what time it is. What I don't like is polishin' the bell. Or the binnacle." He stopped for a quick breath. "I wish Captain Woolsey would stop rubbin' that binnacle. Soon's I get it polished up, he fouls it again."

Will clapped him on the shoulder. "Would you rather be mucking out the bilge?" Before Rankin could answer, he added, "Things will liven up once the shooting starts."

"I wish that'd be tomorrow!" Rankin said. "I've been on this brig for nearly a year and nothing excitin' has happened. I'm prayin' the captain assigns me to the long gun when it does!"

CHAPTER NINE

War Is Declared

June 1812

On June 18, 1812, the United States declared war against Great Britain. *Oneida* was off Oswego at the lower eastern end of Lake Ontario when the news reached Captain Woolsey six days later. He patted his sword, suppressed a smile, and heaved a big sigh. His brig and his men had prepared well for this day. They were ready. Except for one thing. They had not received the 32-pound cannonballs he had ordered for the long gun.

He gathered the men around him. "The war has officially begun!" Woolsey said. "We're heading home to Sackets Harbor."

"Huzzah!" Rankin shouted.

The older crew members grinned at Rankin's unreserved excitement.

"Aye!" said one of them, raising his fist into the air. "We're ready!" said another. "Let's go get them!"

Along the way back to Sackets Harbor, the captain pondered what lay ahead. "We'll be fighting the Canadian Provincial Marine," he said to Lieutenant Wells. "Engaging the King's ships, commanded by his officers. They have guns. Lots of guns." He sighed. "We have a three-ton long gun—and no cannonballs that fit it."

"But we have determination!" Wells replied.

The captain nodded in agreement. "We'll have our hands full," he said. "I expect a victory, but it won't come easy."

When *Oneida* and her crew were placed on high alert, Rankin could scarcely contain himself. He pestered his brother with questions. "How soon will the fightin' start? How many British ships will come across the lake? Will their ships be bigger than *Oneida?* Will we shoot them afore they shoot us? Will we—"

"Hush up!" Will said. "You're stirred up like a swarm of bees. Nobody can answer your questions. Just pay attention to Captain Woolsey and do what you're told!"

Rankin kept his mouth shut, but excitement danced in his eyes.

"I'm gonna be a powder monkey in a real battle," he said.

Will looked at him and shook his head. "Don't get too excited. Our war hasn't even started." He looked straight into his eyes and added, "And when it does start, it's not going to be a picnic!"

Rankin tried to calm down, but inside he was as stirred up as a disturbed hornet's nest.

Meanwhile, *Lord Nelson* lay safely tucked away out of sight inside the harbor. *Oneida* returned home to Sackets Harbor, but remained out in Black River Bay.

She set sea watches.

Posted lookouts.

Loaded guns.

Swung to her anchor—and waited for the British to show up.

CHAPTER TEN

Moving the Long Gun

July 1812

By now the schooner *Julia* had transported the long gun to Sackets Harbor, along with three 6-pounders.

"We'll arm *Lord Nelson* with the lighter guns," Woolsey said to Lieutenant Wells. "But first we must get that long gun off *Julia*." He thumbed his chin as he considered how to do that. "Any warship sent down from Canada would expect to face battle on the water," he mused. "Our long gun could deliver quite a surprise from atop the bluff."

"Not only a surprise, but a wicked whack as well!" Lieutenant Wells said.

Captain Woolsey rolled his shoulders. "It will take all the strong backs we can muster to haul it up there." He looked straight at his lieutenant. "We have no idea when the British will attack. We must get help from ashore and get that gun up there post-haste."

Lieutenant Wells nodded. He understood the need to hurry. Off he went to set the crew to the task of hoisting the gun out of the *Julia*.

"Kin I help, too?" Rankin asked.

Wells appreciated the lad's enthusiasm. "Come along," he said.

The captain issued a call for help and dozens of villagers reported. Runners were sent out to call in the militiamen. Some of them showed up along with men from Captain Elisha Camp's artillery unit.

Inch by inch the huge cannon was hoisted from *Julia* and moved ashore. Then every available man pitched in to help drag the monster up the hill to the edge of the bluff.

"I want to help, too," Rankin said. He and Will struggled right along with the others, grunting, groaning, and straining at the task.

By the time they reached the top, the men were gasping for breath.

Rankin rolled his eyes at Will and breathed deeply. "I didn't expect it to be so hard."

Will gave him a gentle elbow jab. "You did good."

After a brief break, the men mounted the heavy gun on a previously constructed pivot. Rankin and Will joined the others in raising their blistered hands in triumph.

"HUZZAH! HUZZAH!"

Their lusty shouts drifted across the lake.

The shouting died down, and the tired men collapsed on the ground, ready for a long rest.

Their work was not yet finished. Now that the 32-pounder was in place, Captain Woolsey wanted the smaller guns on *Julia* moved to the shore battery, as well. "Those 6-pounders can cause more damage from up here than on *Lord Nelson,*" he said. "We'll use them and the long gun to stop Great Britain's attack. Later, when Sackets Harbor is safe, we'll mount them on *Lord Nelson.*"

The winded men turned their heads away and rolled their eyes. So what if the 6-ers were much lighter? Every one of their muscles ached. Rest was what they wanted, not more heavy work.

"You've done a hard job this day and done it well," Woolsey said.

"There will be an extra tot of rum for each man."

The crew brightened at the news, though powder boys did not get rum and Will, as often as not, gave his ration to his messmates.

"I know you're tired. Haul those 6-pounders up here. Then you can quit."

The weary men struggled to their feet, stretched their muscles, and went back to *Julia*.

Rankin pitched in to help as the smaller guns were hoisted up to the cliff. He was proud to have lent a hand, especially with moving the 32-pounder. He spoke to Will under his breath. "I sure hope I git to carry the powder charges to the long gun!"

The next day Rankin's section had the morning watch. As was the custom, they had come on duty a few minutes before the hour. A rooster in the village greeted the dawn as Rankin turned the glass and struck the bell.

BONG-BONG! BONG-BONG! BONG-BONG! BONG-BONG!

The bosun's mate on watch wrote in the rough log: "04:00, 19 July 1812, wind freshening, now east-northeast, force 5."

Oneida's pitching motion had increased. She was feeling the chop.

Shortly, from the masthead, came a hail: "Deck there. Sail Ho!"

Ford bellowed back, "Where away?"

"Sou'west . . . many sail . . . out between Stony and Galloo."

The shout from the lookout startled Rankin. "Is the fight really startin'?" he asked.

"It looks like it," said Will.

In a flash Captain Woolsey appeared on deck. Lieutenant Wells came up, rubbing sleep from his eyes. He'd gone below when the watch changed, barely two hours earlier. He buttoned his coat against the morning chill. "That will be the Kingston Squadron," Woolsey said, buckling his sword belt. He rested his hand on the hilt of his sword. "Mister Ford," he said to the officer of the watch, "get us underway, if you please."

"Aye, aye, Sir," said the Sailing Master.

Shortly thereafter the bosun's mate raised his pipe and played a shrill tune to call *Oneida's* off-watch crew to duty. The men tumbled from their hammocks and rushed to their stations. Having been well drilled, some of the seamen went aloft, and some to their line-handling assignments.

Others tailed onto the anchor cable. At the bosun's command, they grasped the cable and hauled.

Raising the anchor was grueling work, made slightly easier by the windlass. "Too bad we don't have a capstan on this brig," said the bosun. He rolled his shoulder muscles and took a deep breath. "But, to make room for all that machinery on deck, we'd have to eliminate two carronades."

Sailing Master Ford gave a series of commands:

"Set jib and spanker."

Oneida slowly moved up over her anchor.

"Anchor's aweigh" came the cry from the bow.

"Loose tops'ls," Master Ford ordered. "Steer nor'west by north."

"Steer nor'west by north, aye," repeated the helmsman.

The brig came around and headed toward Pillar Point. More sails were set as *Oneida* moved farther out into Black River Bay.

The lookout had spotted British sails catching the rays of the rising sun. Captain Woolsey leapt into the ratlines to see for himself. He steadied his long glass. The enemy vessels were now clearly visible. Five of them!

He focused on the leading one. She was ship-rigged and flying the flag of the commander. "It's *Royal George*," he said.

Oneida fired a gun to alert those ashore. The British were coming. Woolsey signaled, "An enemy is approaching on the lake."

Alarm guns boomed, and messengers raced into the countryside to carry the news.

With all of the excitement on board the brig, Rankin almost forgot to turn the glass.

BONG-BONG! BONG-BONG! Six a.m.

As *Oneida* sailed back and forth across the bay, Woolsey watched the oncoming fleet's maneuverings. A stiff breeze chilled the back of his neck. The enemy was slowly but steadily closing the distance. Without a doubt, an attack on Sackets Harbor was about to take place.

"Hands to breakfast if you please, Mr. Wells."

"An' it's high time, too," Rankin muttered.

CHAPTER ELEVEN

"Surrender your ships!"

Mid-morning July 19, 1812

"Mr. Wells, call the crew to quarters."

"Aye, aye, Sir."

Pipes sounded and petty officers shouted. The men formed several lines in front of their captain. Woolsey had their full attention as he read a letter from the British commander, Hugh Earl, that had been brought aboard by a messenger.

To Colonel Christopher Bellinger:

We're coming for Lord Nelson *and* Oneida.

You must surrender both vessels to us.

Refuse and we will destroy your village!

Hugh Earl, Commander, Royal George

Woolsey nodded his permission.

The men hooted.

"He can't make us give up our ships!"

"We'll take care of Earl!"

"Just let him show his face!"

Captain Woolsey smiled and gave his sword hilt a hearty slap. He nodded to Lieutenant Wells, and the men were dismissed.

"But what about their threat? What if they come an' set the village afire?" Rankin asked.

"You've no cause to fret over something that's not going to happen," Will said. "Look at Captain Woolsey. Does he look worried?"

If the captain was concerned, he never showed it. But he had to make his battle plans quickly. "The British squadron's got 70 guns against our 18!" he said to Lieutenant Wells. "But our men are well trained and we are faster than those tubs. We could use both our broadsides to good effect if we could get amongst them."

Wells replied, "Aye, Sir. And once there, we could go out into the lake. But that'd leave the harbor defenseless."

"Not defenseless, Mr.Wells. Don't forget the battery on the cliff."

The time for talk was over. Woolsey had reached his decision. He needed to outwit the British. "Commander Earl must know that our militia is on the bluff," he said to Lieutenant Wells. "I'll wager he doesn't know we have a 32-pounder up there."

"If we lured them close enough, he'd soon find out!"

"I've been thinking the same thing." The captain cast a glance down the bay. "The wind has backed to the north. That will move them along faster." Turning toward Wells he said, "Bring us close to shore near the mouth of the harbor. We'll moor the brig there."

"Aye, aye, Sir."

"Once you're moored, make haste to get the starboard guns ashore and up on the bluff. If Earl comes 'round past the battery, we'll use the larboard guns to deny him the harbor."

Woolsey's crew set to work and made it happen.

"Mr. Wells, stay here and fight the brig if they get this far. I'm going to the battery. I'll return if I hear your guns."

"Aye, aye, Sir!"

He turned toward Will. "You're a steady man, McMullin, and a good leader. I want you as gun captain on the long gun. Pick two of your mates to go with you and report to the battery. You can add to your crew from the militia."

Will knuckled his forehead in a quick salute. "Beg pardon, Sir," he sputtered, his face clouded with doubt.

"I'll be up there with you," Woolsey said.

Will paled at the weighty responsibility.

Woolsey drew back in surprise. "You know more about guns than most anyone else on this brig. So what if you've never fired a 32-pounder? You've been drilling with those carronades here on deck. Firing the long gun is not that different." He paused. "I'll show you what to do. Then you can take over and teach the others." He looked Will in the eye. "I need a steady hand in charge of that gun. If I didn't think you could handle the job, I wouldn't send you up there."

Will McMullin, local farmer turned sailor, flushed at his captain's praise. He straightened his shoulders, and gulped. "Thank y— Aye, aye, Sir!"

Woolsey turned to Rankin with a twinkle in his eyes. "I need a good powder boy today."

A broad smile split Rankin's face. He and his brother would be working together on the long gun crew. His heart thumped in his chest like a drummer's beat to quarters. "Aye!"

Rankin's courage under fire would soon be tested, but not on *Oneida* as he had dreamed. He wouldn't mind. Ever since he'd heard about that long gun, he'd wanted to be a part of its crew. He lost little time in getting himself up to the bluff.

And so they prepared. And waited.

CHAPTER TWELVE

Battle Preparations

As the British fleet advanced toward the harbor, the wind backed more westerly. Now it was coming from behind them. They moved faster as they approached the dangerous lee shore. In such tight quarters, the vessels risked being blown onto the rocks. Or colliding with one another. Perhaps that was what Earl was thinking.

Captain Woolsey observed that only *Royal George* came close. What kind of strategy was that, he wondered.

He hastened to the battery on the cliff to gather his forces. Though this battle was being waged from a bluff rather than on the water, it was still his to command. When Captain Camp and his men arrived, dragging two 9-pounder field guns, Woolsey directed him to manage his own men and their guns.

The captain had promised to help Will with the long gun. Will had brought Hugh Paul with him from the brig. Hugh was a friend who had enlisted on the same day as Will and Rankin. Because he was also from the village, the local men would likely work well with him.

Woolsey began to bark orders. "McMulllin needs a few more men for his long gun crew!" He nodded toward Black Julius, a local person of color, standing nearby. "You," he said.

Black Julius stepped forward.

Captain Camp assigned Sergeant Thomas D. Spicer from his artillerymen to work with Will.

Woolsey focused on Rankin dancing around the long gun. "Your job is to carry our powder charges up from the brig." He looked around as if to see if everything was organized and then added. "You'd better be off!"

"Aye, aye, Sir!"

Rankin scrambled down from the bluff to *Oneida*. He charged across the gangplank and bounded down the ladders to the magazine where the gunner's mate was waiting. Rankin pushed the wet curtain aside and grabbed the bucket of charges held out for him. He turned, clambered back up the ladders and raced for the bluff as fast as his legs would carry him.

As he trudged up the hill the second time, Captain Camp stopped him. He pointed toward the blockhouse. "There's a large store of powder over there, and we have permission to use it. You can get your charges there." He glanced at the long gun and then back at Rankin.

"Thank'ee, Sir."

Rankin set his re-refilled bucket down at a safe distance from the battery and waited for orders.

War was a new experience for many of the villagers. The activity on the bluff was so frightening to some men that they fled into the woods, taking their families with them. Others were glad the war was finally beginning. The brave and curious ones hung around with their wives and children, waiting to see what might happen.

Meanwhile Will's men gathered around the long gun. They had helped haul it up to the bluff, but how to load it was a mystery. True to his word, Captain Woolsey took charge. With great patience he explained the procedure step by step.

Will watched him like a hungry hawk spotting its prey, not missing a single word or movement. As gun captain, he would make sure everything was done right. His final chore before firing was to prime the cannon. That meant pouring fine gunpowder into the vent at the near end of the barrel. He would assign the other jobs to members of his crew.

"Rankin, you need to bring more powder charges when I ask for them."

Rankin beamed. "Aye, aye!"

"Black Julius, you'll put the charges into the gun and ram them into place with this long pole. I'll show you how to do that." He looked at Hugh Paul. "Your job is to stick this carpenter's awl through the vent and poke a hole in the top powder bag. When I give the signal, apply the slow-match to light the powder."

Will chose Sergeant Spicer and two of Captain Camp's men to load the heavy cannonballs. Before reloading, another of Camp's men would use a wet sponge to snuff out any sparks that remained after the firing. That would keep the new powder charge from being set off as the gun was loaded.

The crew wouldn't know until they fired if the heavy gun needed to be raised, lowered, or turned. Although it was on a pivot, it would still take everyone's muscle to move it in any direction.

"Stand back before we fire," Will warned. "That gun will jump! The blast will shoot out wadding and scraps of burning flannel from the powder bags."

The men fumbled through their first practice runs as each learned his job and when to do it. They were catching on, but they fretted over not having 32-pound cannonballs.

"We'll have to make do with 24-pound balls." Woolsey frowned as he spoke. "It's hard enough to get a hit with balls that fit. A 24-pound shot fired from a 32-pound cannon is inaccurate." He shook his head in frustration. "If we could wrap those smaller balls in something to make them larger, it would improve our chances of blasting *Royal George*."

Captain Camp's wife Sofia and her best friend Abby Vaughan had been standing nearby with other women from the village waiting to see what would happen. They were within earshot when Capt. Woolsey made his comment. Mrs. Vaughan took a long look at the big gun and then at

Mrs. Camp. "Can't we find something to do that?"

"I know something we might use," said Mrs. Camp.

"So do I," said Mrs. Vaughan. "Let's go get it!"

With that, the women were off down the hill to their nearby homes as fast as they could run, being careful not to trip on their long, bulky skirts.

CHAPTER THIRTEEN

Women at War

Captain Woolsey opened his long glass and studied the British fleet from the bluff, now advancing between the tip of Pillar Point and Horse Island. They were entering the bay and coming closer. Did they really think he would give up two ships?

The captain closed the glass and turned about just as the women reappeared carrying a couple of thread-bare blankets.

Wide-eyed, Rankin watched them tear one of the blankets into narrow strips. Mrs. Camp laid a stack of two or three of them on the ground.

"I'll roll the ball onto the strips," said Mrs. Vaughan. "You hold it in place while I pick up the ends and start wrapping."

Mrs. Camp reached out to steady the 24-pound ball, but it rolled away from her. She grabbed for it and rolled it back onto the flannel. As soon as she wrapped it a bit, the heavy ball rolled away again. She caught it and tried once more. She could not keep it still long enough to wrap it. Frustrated, she turned to Rankin, who stood nearby. "Help us steady this cannonball!"

Rankin refused to help. "That's not my job! I'm a powder monkey," he sputtered.

Abby Vaughan placed a firm hand on Rankin's shoulder and glared into his eyes. "That long gun needs cannonballs that fit. You ARE going to help us wrap this one!"

Rankin lowered his head, too ashamed to look at her. He dropped to his knees and steadied the ball.

With his help, the women wrapped it until it had grown into the size of a coconut. Mrs. Vaughan rolled it over to Sergeant Spicer.

When she turned from him, Rankin escaped back to where the men were working with the huge gun.

Still unsure of himself, each man took his time with his part in loading the cannon. When he was given the nod, Rankin handed the powder charges to Black Julius, who pushed them as far back as they would go into the muzzle. Will stood by as Julius rammed a wad in on top of the bags. Sergeant Spicer directed two militiamen in rolling the wrapped ball into the barrel of the gun. Black Julius rammed home another wad to hold everything in place. Hugh Paul pushed the awl into the vent and pierced the top powder bag. Will primed the gun and moved away.

Hugh stood by with slow-match in hand, awaiting the order to light the powder.

Meanwhile, the British fleet edged closer.

"I'll tell you when they are in range," Captain Woolsey said.

"Aye, Sir."

Will's eyes were glued to the vessels.

The smaller ones hung back, but *Royal George,* the flagship, kept coming on. Before long she appeared right in front of the long gun.

"Fire when ready, McMullin!"

"Stand by...__FIRE!" Will bellowed.

Hugh Paul touched the burning rope to the priming powder. As the fire streaked down the trail of powder, he clamped his leather thumb pad over the vent to prevent flashback.

BOOOOM!

A deafening explosion ripped the air.

Every member of the gun crew felt the boom in his chest. Too late, people clapped their hands over their ears. Thick smoke blackened the area in front of the gun. Scraps of burning flannel and shreds of the wads peppered the bluff.

With a sizzling splash the hot ball landed astern of *Royal George.*

"Ooooooh!" A collective groan rose up from the battery.

"DAMMIT!" Will shook his head in disbelief.

The gun crew grimaced.

"That's a good start," Captain Woolsey said. "A moving target's hard to hit. Reload your gun!"

"Aye, aye, Sir!"

The blast had missed *Royal George,* but must have surprised the British commander and his officers. Because of their location, the battery above them was out of sight. They could not raise their heavy "smashers" high enough to reach the long gun on the bluff. When their carronades returned fire with their 32-pound balls, their shots thudded against the cliffs below the bluff, breaking up rocks.

As the firing continued, Rankin kept alert, ready to run for more powder. When it was needed, he charged off to the blockhouse as fast as his legs could carry him.

Meanwhile the women struggled to wrap the 24-pound balls. They succeeded without Rankin's help, but it took longer. As soon as they finished wrapping a ball, one of Captain Camp's men carried it to the long gun. In the meantime, Will's gun crew fired one or two unwrapped balls.

Rankin avoided the women. He needed to be ready to run whenever Will called for more powder.

Royal George closed the range and somehow managed to elevate her carronades a bit. An hour or so into the battle, one of their cannonballs bounded up onto the bluff and bounced inland. Another followed it shortly thereafter. Neither ball caused any damage. When they stopped rolling, Captain Camp's men pried them loose, rolled them onto scraps of canvas, and dragged them to the battery. They had become misshapen when they hit the cliff and would have to be filed down to fit into the long gun.

Before either of them could be fired back at the enemy, a third 32-pound ball flew over the bluff.

CHAPTER FOURTEEN

The Battle Ends

The British 32-pound ball struck the earth, bounded, and rolled down the hill. It plowed a deep furrow into the dooryard of the Vaughan home before coming to a stop.

"That's just what we need!" Sergeant Spicer yelled. He grabbed a spade and sprinted down the hill after it. Shoveling as fast as he could, he dug the dirt away from the ball and dragged it back to the long gun.

"Here's another one for you!" Spicer yelled to Will. "A gift from Commander Earl!"

Rankin tore off to get the powder charges as the gun crew prepared to load the first cannonball of the right size. He returned and handed the powder to Black Julius.

Julius grabbed the powder bags and stuffed them down the muzzle. Two militiamen loaded the heavy ball. Hugh pricked the closest bag through the vent. Will primed the gun.

All was ready.

Royal George moved in closer. Her cannonballs screamed but she was still unable to cause panic on the bluff. After several attempts she gave up. Her captain tacked again and headed back out into the bay.

Will squinted along the barrel just as *Royal George* steadied on her new course.

"Stand by...___FIRE!"

Hugh held the burning rope to the vent, lit the priming powder, and clamped his leather thumb pad over it.

BOOOOOOM!

The British ball was sent home in a mighty blast of smoke and fire.

The long gun crew watched to see where the shot landed and what it did to the departing British flagship.

NOTHING!

Not even a splash!

How could they have missed again?

Did the ball fly all the way across the bay to Pillar Point?

Perhaps it had gone through the rigging, landing on the other side.

As the roar of the long gun faded, an eerie silence crept over the bluff.

They gun crew stared at *Royal George* and shook their heads.

Down in the bay, signal flags appeared on the flagship. Commander Earl was calling for retreat.

The warship sailed out into the bay, heading for Lake Ontario and, presumably, for her base in Kingston. The other vessels in the squadron, having fired no shots, followed her lead.

Up on the hill people stood slack-jawed, puzzled by what was happening down in the bay.

"Well, I'll be damned!" Will said. He exchanged bewildered glances with Captain Woolsey and shrugged. It appeared as though his shoulders were paralyzed as he kept his focus on the fleeing squadron. "We had enough powder to destroy *Royal George.*"

Captain Woolsey nodded in agreement. "I'm not sure we even hit her!"

Will threw up his hands in frustration. "We certainly didn't hurt the other vessels. They were never in close enough range for us to fire upon them."

Captain Camp shook his head as if to shake away his consternation. "My men have had no experience with a moving target," he said. He glanced toward them as they stood about, looking as perplexed as the gun crew. "They held their fire, waiting to see what would happen."

Rankin was as baffled as everyone else. He looked at Will and asked, "Why did the *Royal George* give up?"

"Who knows?" Will said. He glanced toward the captain and Lieutenant Wells. "It looks like Captain Woolsey wonders the same thing."

The sudden departure of the enemy left every person on the bluff perplexed.

Why did Commander Earl give up the fight?

No one knew the answer, but at the moment it didn't matter.

Captain Woolsey broke the silence. "Sackets Harbor is safe!"

The battery erupted in shouts of victory. Men raised their fists in triumph.

"HUZZAH! HUZZAH! HUZZAH!"

"HUZZAH!" Rankin yelled, his voice joining with the others.

The British had not captured *Oneida*.

Had not taken back *Lord Nelson*.

Had not burned Sackets Harbor.

The entire village cheered as their fleeing enemy faded from view.

"Congratulations, men!" said Captain Woolsey. "You've done well!"

Three of Camp's militiamen took up their fifes, and an old veteran came out of the tavern with his fiddle in hand. A militia drummer boy joined the hastily assembled band. Everyone on the bluff whooped it up as the group played "Yankee Doodle" over and over again.

Rankin grabbed Will's hand and raised it in triumph as they celebrated with the others. They had joined up on *Oneida,* helped defend their village, and watched the British turn tail.

Though it seemed much longer, the struggle had lasted only about two hours. In some mysterious way, the Americans had bested a much stronger foe. Strange as it was, this was still a day of victory. A day for celebration.

Captain Woolsey stared out over Black River Bay, alone with his thoughts amidst the hubbub. His hand rested firmly on the hilt of his sword. The war was not over. Though they had successfully defended Sackets Harbor, the village was not safe from another British attack.

He had lost none of his men, and not one had been injured. It had been a day of victory, and for that he was grateful.

The British fleet had returned to Canada, but they would be back. It was his responsibility to be prepared.

Rankin couldn't stop smiling. "I did my job, too!" he boasted. "If I hadn't brung the powder charges, the long gun couldn't have scared the *Royal George* away."

Will slapped him on the shoulder. "Right!" he said. "Let's go find Pa."

Rankin McMullin, of the U.S. Brig *Oneida*, would forever remember this day, July 19, 1812, when his dream of being a powder monkey came true.

AFTERWORD
Why Did the British Retreat?

The people of Sackets Harbor celebrated their victory with great joy. To them it was a miracle, like David bringing down Goliath. Nobody but Hugh Earl knew why he had called a retreat. Back home in Kingston, few people took notice of his failed attack on Lake Ontario, and he chose not to explain his actions. A brief comment in the *Kingston Gazette* called it "an honorable effort." That was the only mention made of it by the British.

Researchers have developed a credible theory for the silence. Sir George Prevost was Great Britain's Governor General of Canada at this time. When it became clear that war would break out, he feared losing territory. He also worried about his impulsive senior officers, men like Hugh Earl, the commander of the Provincial Marine. Though Earl's ships were not part of the Royal Navy, they were armed and dangerous. To keep all his officers under control, Sir George issued orders forbidding offensive action against America.

Major General Isaac Brock commanded all His Majesty's forces in Upper Canada. He wanted to attack Sackets Harbor as soon as war was declared. Earl knew that the Royal Navy was apt to take over the fight on the Great Lakes. If that happened, he would be out of a job. A victory at Sackets Harbor would strengthen his position, and perhaps he could become an officer of the Royal Navy.

Governor General Prevost's order prevented General Brock from carrying out his plan, but the Canadian Provincial Marine was not under Prevost's direct command. It's doubtful that Earl would have been so bold as to have acted on his own. Dr. Gary Gibson, respected researcher of the war on the lakes, says it's more likely Earl did not receive Prevost's orders. It's possible that Earl's superior saw him as merely running an army transport system and never suspected him to try anything so aggressive.

If Earl attacked Sackets Harbor, Brock would get what he wanted. If the attack was successful, both he and General Brock would benefit. If the attack was not successful, Brock could not be blamed, as there is no evidence he knew what Earl was about to do.

Earl had nothing to lose so he attacked. But the guns on *Royal George* couldn't reach the bluff. His mission failed. He might as well go home.

What Happened after the First Battle?

Sackets Harbor had become Lake Ontario's fortified naval base with the arrival of the gun-brig *Oneida* in November 1810. Thereafter, Army troops were sent to protect the base. After the attack on July 19, 1812, it served as the headquarters for American naval and military activity on Lake Ontario. In late August, the Secretary of the Navy ordered Captain Isaac Chauncey to proceed to Sackets Harbor to construct a fleet to protect Lake Ontario from invasion by Canada.

After Chauncey's arrival in October, thousands of soldiers, sailors, and marines flocked to the village. Their task was to build that fleet and prepare for an attack on Montreal. The new arrivals were housed near Fort Tompkins at Smith's Cantonment.

Many of the workers were skilled shipbuilders. Some built small schooners and huge frigates. Others converted merchant vessels to gunboats. They worked in the wilderness in harsh winter weather. And they worked fast. Two frigates went from standing timber to launching in record time: The *Madison* with her 24 guns took six weeks, and the *Mohawk* with her 42 guns was built in only five weeks. The 58-gun *Superior* was finished between the building of the two others.

Great Britain attacked again on May 29, 1813. This time her mission was to destroy the shipyards. She failed. Then the war moved to other fronts.

After the war ended in December 1814, the Lake Ontario fleet was placed in storage. Major naval activities at Sackets Harbor had come to an end. Fort Tompkins fell into ruins and was eventually torn down to make way for the construction of a new army post.

Later Developments

1816   Construction of Madison Barracks, named in honor of the 4th President of the United States, begins just north of the village. Once completed, the Barracks serve as a training post until 1946.

1817   Agreement between the United States and Great Britain limits all naval forces on the Great Lakes.

1826-1838	Old shipyard buildings, including Fort Tompkins, are demolished.
1848-1849	New quarters are built for the Navy commandant and lieutenant.
1861-1865	Madison Barracks serves as a recruiting center for the Civil War.
After 1918	The Barracks becomes a hospital post following WWI.
1946	All military activities cease at Madison Barracks.
1955	The Navy Yard and Navy Point are turned over to the Town of Hounsfield.
1966	The Navy Yard becomes the present- day Sackets Harbor Battlefield State Historic Site.

Today, the U.S. National Park Service lists Sackets Harbor as one of the nation's top ten War of 1812 sites. Community support enables the site to interpret the past, while improving the character of the village and surrounding areas. From Memorial Day through Labor Day, guides act out camp life, dressed in military uniforms like those worn during the war.

During one weekend each summer, a battle reenactment takes place. A schedule of battlefield activities is posted at www.sacketsharborbattlefield.org.

Battle Folklore

Two widespread tales drew me to this battle. Later I learned they had no foundation in truth. The first myth concerns the 32-pounder long gun. Some writers stated that the gun was called "Old Sow" because it was dug out of the mud and then set up to fight the battle. The truth is the gun was probably cast a few years earlier. It was brought from Oswego to Sackets Harbor soon after war was declared.

The second absorbing tale was about wrapping the too-small cannonballs. Some writers say they had been wrapped in pieces of carpets from the Vaughan and Camp homes. That is unlikely in that era because carpets were hard to come by and hard to replace. Would those women have given them up so easily? I don't think so. But parting with their worn-out blankets was no great sacrifice.

My research turned up some other creative ideas on how the battle was fought. Tales of the destruction by the battery on the hill are varied, vivid, and undocumented by reliable sources. My battle description is

based on conclusions drawn by researchers who studied the war for years.

Acknowledgements

Constance Barone, Site Manager, Sackets Harbor Battlefield State Historic Site: Instigator and cheerleader in the creation of this story

Gary M. Gibson, Ph.D., Sackets Harbor researcher and authority on the Naval War of 1812 on Lake Ontario: Supplier of information who graciously vetted my manuscript

Robert and Jeannie Brennan, Town of Hounsfield and Village of Sackets Harbor Historians: Encouragers along the way who gave me access to their huge private library on the War of 1812

Burt Phillips, Retired teacher: Chief authority on all things naval, and my astute copyeditor

Lorraine Caramanna, 6th-8th grade English teacher at Lyme Central School, Chaumont, NY, and Lynn Kellogg and Heather Dunning, 6th grade teachers at South Jefferson Central Middle School, Adams, NY: Educators who shared the manuscript with their students and provided valuable feedback from their perspective

Nellie Mae Schauer: Meticulous proofreader

Aline Newman, Jean Capron, Jeanne Converse, and Judyann Grant: Members of my supportive Critique Group who wouldn't let me get by with anything less than my best

Nancy Morrison: Map maker and encourager

Lyrisse Castro Grube: Front Cover

Sonya Marie Boushek: Back Cover

Arthur Wakefield Marston: My supportive husband, confidant, and anchor for more than fifty years

Find Out More about the War and Life at Sea

Campbell, Carole R. *The Powder Monkey.* (Young American Series #4) Shippensburg, PA: White Mane Books, 1999.

Carter, Alden R. *The War of 1812: Second Fight for Independence.* New York, NY: Franklin Watts, 1992.

Childress, Diana. *The War of 1812.* (Chronicle of America's Wars) Minneapolis, MN: Lerner, 2004.

Forester, C.S. *Captain Horatio Hornblower.* New York, NY: Little Brown, 1939.

Gay, Kathlyn and Martin Gay. *War of 1812.* (Voices from the Past) New York, NY: Twenty-First Century Books, 1995.

Greeson, Janet. *An American Army of Two.* Minneapolis, MN: Carolrhoda, 1991.

Ibbitson, John. *Jeremy's War 1812.* Toronto, ON: Kids Can Press, 2000.

Kipling, Rudyard. *Captains Courageous.* New York, NY: The Book League of America, 1897.

Muller, Charles Geoffrey. *Hero of Two Seas: The Story of Midshipman Thomas Macdonough.* New York, NY: David McKay, 1968.

Platt, Richard and Stephen Biesty. *Stephen Biesty's Cross-Sections: Man-Of-War.* New York: Dorling Kindersley, 1993.

Rand, Gloria and Ted Rand. *Sailing Home: A Story of a Childhood at Sea.* New York, NY: North South Books, 2001.

Ransom, Candice. *Flames in the City: A Tale of the War of 1812.* (Time Spies) Renton, WA: Mirrorstone, 2008.

Pearson, Kit. *Whispers of War: The War of 1812 Diary of Susanna Merritt.* (Dear Canada) Toronto, Canada: Scholastic Canada, 2002.

Sanchez, Anita. *The Invasion of Sandy Bay.* Honesdale, PA: Calkins Creek, 2008.

TERMS YOU WILL MEET

Anchor's aweigh—A term meaning the anchor is off the bottom and the vessel is free to maneuver.

Armourer—A man who maintains and repairs firearms.

Battery—A group of guns in one location, used for combined action.

Bilge—The lowest part of a ship's hull. Water from leaks, rain, and spray collects there, making it a filthy, foul-smelling place. The water has to be pumped out and the rest mucked out.

Binnacle—A box mounted on a post that houses the ship's compass.

Blocks—Wooden casings that enclose the pulleys.

Boatswain—(Also bos'n). A petty officer in charge of a ship's rigging, anchors, cables, and sails.

Bow—The front end of the vessel.

Brig—A two-masted sailing vessel with square sails on both masts.

Broadside—All the guns able to fire on one side of a warship, or the action of firing all the guns on one side. This may occur all together or in rapid succession as the enemy moves into the aiming point of the gun.

Carronade—A gun that is shorter and lighter than a cannon (long gun) and mounted on a slide instead of a wheeled carriage. It has a smaller gun crew but fires the same size balls to a shorter range. These guns were called "smashers" because of the effect their low velocity balls had on wooden ships.

Cutter—A small, lightly armed, patrol boat with a single mast.

Flagship—The ship that carries the commander of a fleet and displays his flag.

Gangway—A narrow walkway along either side of the upper deck.

Hull—The main body of a ship.

Jib—A triangular sail rigged from the foremast to the bow of a vessel.

Larboard—The left side of the ship as one faces forward. This term has been replaced by "port."

Long glass—An early telescope.

Long gun—A heavy, mounted cannon, nine or ten feet long. The one used in this battle weighed three tons and fired cannonballs weighing thirty-two pounds.

Magazine—The area of a vessel built below the waterline where the gun powder is stored.

Masthead—The highest point on a mast. The lookout is just below it.

Militia—A military unit of citizens called up in an emergency.

Petty officer—A non-commissioned officer.

Port—A modern name for larboard.

Potash—Chemical obtained by leaching the ashes of burned trees. During the early 1800s, it was sold to the British for making gunpowder and other things.

Powder boys—Swift young boys who carried bags of powder charges from the magazine to the guns during a battle. These boys were trained to become seamen after a couple of years. They were smaller and more agile than the adults, making it easier for them to move around the action rather than running into it. With their limited skills, they were more expendable than trained seamen.

Powder monkeys—A nickname for powder boys because they were small and nimble like monkeys.

Schooner—A relatively small sailing vessel with triangular sails on two or more masts.

Ship-rigged vessel—A three-masted sailing vessel with square sails on all masts.

Ship's bell—A signaling device used to warn other vessels and the crew of danger. It also tells the crew the time. The number of strikes marks the passage of each half-hour in a four-hour watch. Striking the bells was one of Rankin's favorite jobs when on duty.

Skiff—A small light open boat.

Spanker—A triangular or trapezoidal sail on the after-most mast of a square-rigged vessel.

Starboard—The right side of a ship as one faces forward.

Stern—The back end of the vessel.

Thirty-two pounder—A gun made to fire a ball weighing thirty-two pounds.

Topsail—A loose-footed sail hoisted above the others on a mast.

Wad—A mass of canvas or rope fibers stuffed into the barrel of the cannon to hold the gunpowder and the cannonball in place until the cannon is fired.

Watch—A division of time on board ship. Also, a certain portion of a crew assigned to work a given length of time.

Windlass—A device used to wind the cables to bring up the anchor by manpower.

ANNOTATED BIBLIOGRAPHY

Nineteenth Century Sources

Abbott, Willis J. *Blue Jackets of 1812: A History of the Naval Battles of the Second War with Great Britain.* New York: Dodd, Mead, 1887. Many illustrations.

Hough, Franklin B. *A History of Jefferson County in the State of New York from the Earliest Period to the Present Time.* Watertown, NY: Sterling & Ridell, 1854. Pp. 176-178 and 458-464.

Kingston, William Henry Giles. *From Powder Monkey to Admiral: A Story of Naval Adventure.* New York, NY: A. C. Armstrong & Son, 1884. An intriguing tale of life on a privateer with excellent details on the work of each crew member.

Lossing, Benson J. *The Pictorial Field-Book of the War of 1812.* New York: Harper & Brothers, 1868.

Lovett, John. Letter written from Ogdensburg on July 29, 1812, to his friend Joseph Alexander in Albany, concerning the battle of Sackets Harbor on July 19, 1812. Lovett was a lawyer from Troy who became military secretary and aide-de-camp to Major General Stephen van Rensselaer, who was appointed by Gov. Daniel D. Tompkins on July 13, 1812, to take command of the militia on the northern and western frontiers of New York State.

Our Country and Its People: A Descriptive Work on Jefferson County, New York: Boston: Boston History Co., 1898.

Tomlinson, Everett.T. *The Boy Soldiers of 1812.* Boston, MA: Lee and Shepard, 1895.

Woolsey, Melanchton T. "Melancthon Taylor Woolsey's Journals #5," October 11, 1811—February 5, 1812 Oneida County Historical Society, Utica, NY. Woolsey Family Papers, 52. MSS Box 95, WFP.2 JOU.1-5. Handwritten, leatherbound.

Woolsey, Melanchton. Letters from M.T. Woolsey and others that discuss matters concerning Sackets Harbor and what happened on July 19,1812. This information came from the digital research library at the Sackets Harbor Battlefield, beginning with [M148 Roll 9 1812 Vol 1 Item 5] and ending with [M124 Roll 86 1820 Vol 2 Item 113].

Other Sources

Barbuto, Richard V. *Niagara, 1814: America Invades Canada.* Lawrence, Kansas; University Press of Kansas, 2000. P.18. Explains the role of the Provincial Marine in the War of 1812.

Platt, Richard and Stephen Biesty. *Stephen Biesty's Cross-Sections: Man-Of-War.* New York: Dorling Kindersley, 1993.

Brennan, Robert E. and Jeannie. *Sackets Harbor.* (Images of America) Charleston, SC: Arcadia Publishing, 2000.

Brodine, Jr., Charles E., Michael J. Crawford and Christine F. Hughes. *Against All Odds: U.S. Sailors in the War of 1812.* Washington, D.C.: Naval Historical Center. Dept. of Navy, 2004. Good for incidental points on how the war was fought.

Butts, Edward. *Outlaws of the Lakes: Bootlegging and Smuggling from Colonial Times to Prohibition.* Holt, Michigan: Thunder Bay Press, 2004. Pp. 1-41.

Chapelle, Howard Irving. *The History of the American Sailing Navy; the Ships and Their Development.* New York: Bonanza Books (W.W. Norton), 1949.

Dudley, William S. ed. *The Naval War of 1812.* A documentary history. Vol.1. Washington, D.C.: Naval Historical Center, 1985.

Harper's Encyclopedia of United States History from 480 A.D. to 1915. Harper Bros., 1915. Vol. 8, "S" "Sackets Harbor."

Hickey, Donald R. *The War of 1812: A Forgotten Conflict.* Chicago: University of Illinois Press, 1989. (Doesn't mention the first battle).

Hitsman, J. Mackay. *The Incredible War of 1812: A Military History.* Updated by Donald E. Graves. Toronto: Robin Brass Studio, 1965. Canadian perspective.

Landon, Harry F. *The North Country: a History Embracing Jefferson, St. Lawrence, Oswego, Lewis, and Franklin Counties, NY.* Indianapolis: Historical Publishing Co., 1932.

Malcomson, Robert. *Lords of the Lakes.* Annapolis, MD: Naval Institute Press, 1998.

Malcomson, Robert. *Warships of the Great Lakes 1754-1834.* Annapolis, MD: Naval

Institute Press, 2001.

Miller, David. *The World of Jack Aubrey: Twelve-pounders, Frigates,Cutlasses, and Insignia of His Majesty's Royal Navy*. Philadelphia, PA: Courage Books, 2003.

Palmer, Richard F. "James Fennimore Cooper and the Navy Brig *Oneida.*" *Inland Seas*. Published by Great Lakes Historical Society, Vol. 40, No.2, Summer, 1984.

Petrie, Donald A. *The Prize Game: Lawful Looting on the High Seas in the Days of Fighting Sail*. Annapolis, MD: Naval Institute Press, 1999.

Robson, Martin. *Not Enough Room to Swing a Cat: Naval Slang and Its Everyday Use*. Annapolis, MD: Naval Institute Press, 2008.

Rogers, A. E. *Hounsfield Cemetery Inscriptions:Town of Hounsfield, Jefferson County. NY*. Published by Ellen and John Bartlett, 1996. Verification of minuteman Thomas D. Spicer, participant of first Battle of Sackets Harbor. Spicer responded to call up from Sulfur Springs, about six miles away, on morning of 19 April. His description of the battle is recorded in *The Boy Soldiers of 1812* by Tomlinson.

Rubel, David. *Scholastic Timelines: The United States in the 19th Century*. New York, NY: Agincourt Press, 1996. Has a few pages on the War of 1812. Mentions Lucy Brewer a.k.a.Nicholas Baker, but reliable sources say the story is fictitious.

Roosevelt, Theodore. *The Naval War of 1812*. New York, NY: Modern Library, 1999. Pp. 79-87, 123-141, 195-204. A definitive work with lots of statistics.

Skaggs, David Curtis and Gerard Atlof. *A Signal Victory: The Lake Erie Campaign 1812-1813*.Annapolis, MD: Naval Institute Press, 2000. Excellent description of life on board a frigate and what happens during a battle.

Skaggs, David Curtis. *Thomas Macdonough: Master of Command in the Early U.S. Navy*. Annapolis, MD: Naval Institute Press, 2002. Definitive biography and authentic view of life on a frigate.

Stonehouse, Frederick. *Great Lakes Crime II: More Murder, Mayhem, Booze & Broads*. Gwinn, Michigan: Avery Color Studios, 2007. Pp. 65-69.

Taylor, Alan. *The Civil War of 1812: American Citizens, British Subjects, Irish Rebels & Indian Allies*. New York: Knopf, 2010.

Tunis, Edwin. *Oars, Sails and Steam: A Picture Book of Ships*. Baltimore, MD: Johns

Hopkins University Press, 1952. Excellent drawings and inclusive glossary of nautical terms.

Wilder, Patrick. *The Battle of Sackett's Harbour: 1813*. Mount Pleasant, SC: Nautical & Aviation Publishing Company of America, 1994.

Wilder, Patrick and Michael Wilder. *Seaway Trail Guide to the War of 1812*. Oswego, NY: Seaway Trail, 1987. Excellent little illustrated guide.

Internet

Wentling, Mark A. "Capt. Camp's Company of Artillery, New York Militia: Soldiers of First Battle of Sackett's Harbor, 19 July 1812." http://jefferson.nygenweb.net/campsartill.htm

Unpublished Resources

Visited Sackets Harbor Battlefield. Joined the Battlefield Alliance. Used their digital research library. Had access to war correspondence of Melancthon Woolsey. Conducted research in all of their public buildings.

Attended War of 1812 Re-enactments at Sackets Harbor and talked with the re-enactors, August 2, 2008 and August 1, 2009. Attended First Annual War of 1812 Seminar at Ogdensburg, NY, May 2, 2009.

Interviewed Robert and Jeannie Brennan, Town of Hounsfield and Village of Sackets Harbor historians, August 26, 2009.

Had extensive face-to-face and e-mail exchanges with two local men in 2009-2012, Dr. Gary M. Gibson and Burt Phillips.

Gary M. Gibson, Ph.D., resident of Sackets Harbor, has been researching the naval war on Lake Ontario and the St. Lawrence River for more than twenty years. He has presented numerous talks and papers on subject. A second edition of his book, *Service Records of U.S. Navy and Marine Corps Officers Stationed on Lake Ontario during the War of 1812,* was released in March 2012.

Burt Phillips spent his youth on the waters around Sackets Harbor. At one time he lived in the former home of William Vaughan. This background, along with a lifelong interest in naval history and nautical matters, made him an invaluable consultant.

Made in the USA
Charleston, SC
23 July 2012